LITTLE GOLDEN BOOK® CLASSICS
Featuring the art of
Eloise Wilkin

Three Best-Loved Tales

PLAY WITH ME
By Esther Wilkin

❧

SO BIG
By Esther Wilkin

❧

THE BOY WITH A DRUM
By David L. Harrison

A GOLDEN BOOK • NEW YORK
Western Publishing Company, Inc., Racine, Wisconsin 53404

PLAY WITH ME

By Esther Wilkin

Oh, what are the games that Baby plays
With those who love his baby ways?

Creep mouse, creep mouse,
all around town,

Creep mouse, creep mouse,
up and down,

Creep mouse, creep mouse,
in your house,

Creep mouse, creep mouse,

Creep mouse,
Creep mouse,

CREEP mouse!

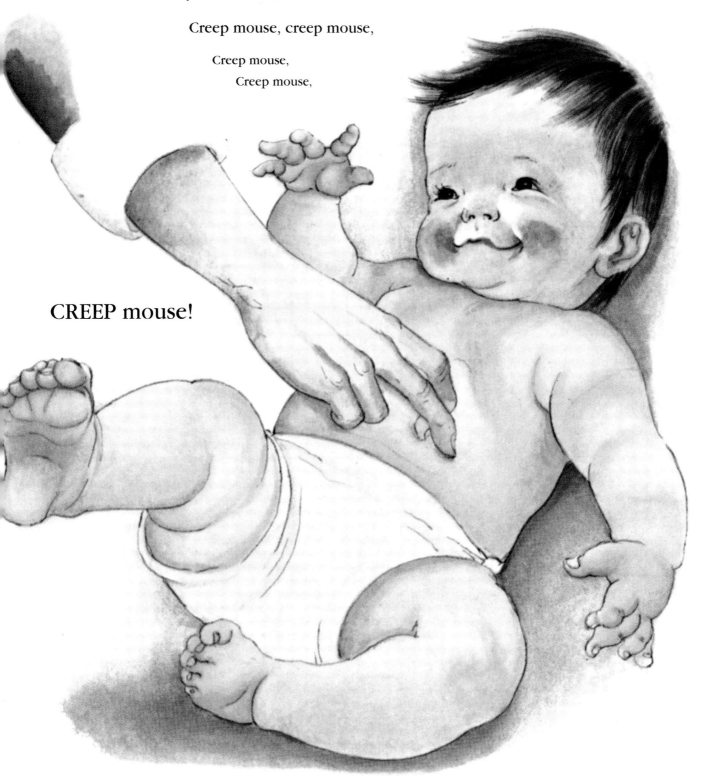

How big is Baby?
SOOOooo big!

Pat-a-cake, pat-a-cake, Baker's Man,
Bake me a cake
   as fast as you can,
Roll it and pat it
   and mark it with "B,"
And put it in the oven
   for Baby and me.

When Baby plays
with an empty pan
and a wooden spoon,
Oh, they can be
most anything!

A little drum
to beat upon,
A soldier hat,
a gun,

A tiny house
   for Mister Mouse,

A great big truck
   to run,

Or just a silver porringer
   to eat a dinner from!

Daddy's foot is a fly-away horse
And Baby's a little man...

UP,
  UP,
    UP
      in
        the
          air
            we
              go,

And DOWN,
    DOWN,
        DOWN again.

Put the ball
    in Daddy's hand,
Take it back again.

Put and take, put and take,
Baby likes to put and take.

Where is Baby hiding?
Where can Baby be?

Peek-a-boo,
my Baby,
I
see
YOU!

Where is
Mommy hiding?
Where can
Mommy be?

Peek-a-boo,
　my Baby,
　　　I
　　　　see
　　　　　YOU!

Rock-a-bye, Baby,
On the treetop,
When the wind blows
The cradle will rock.
When the bough breaks
The cradle will fall.
Down will come Baby,
Cradle and all.

Mommy's arms are a little boat,
A-sailing we will go,
We'll sail-a-boat, sail-a-boat, sail-a-boat fast,
We'll sail-a-boat, sail-a-boat, sail-a-boat slow,

Baby's thumb is Mister Gum,
Next come Peter Point,
Lilly Long, Mrs. Ring,
And Pinky-Little-One.

Down go Peter Point
  and silly Lilly Long,
Down go Mrs. Ring
  and Pinky-Little-One,
And DOWN
  and AROUND
    goes Mister Gum!

This little pig went to market,

This little pig stayed home,

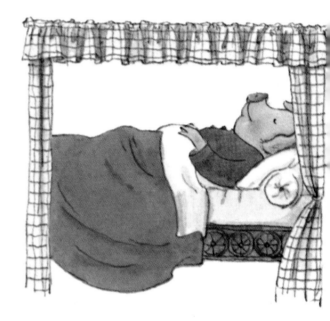

This little pig had roast beef,

This little pig had none,

And this little pig cried
WEE, WEE, WEE,
All the way home.

There's a little round house
With a yellow roof
And two windows upstairs to look out.
There's a latch to loose
And a little red door,
To walk inside, no doubt.

Baby's head is the little house,
His golden hair is the roof,
His eyes are the upstairs windows,
His nose is the latch to loose.
And what do you think
Is the little red door?
Why, Baby's mouth, of course.

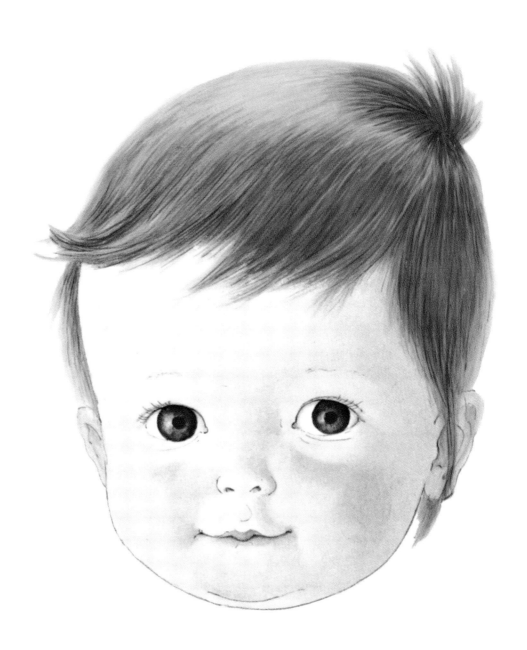

Rock, rock to Boston
To buy a loaf of bread.
Rock, rock home again,
It's time to go to bed.

Mommy makes a shadow picture
High upon the wall,
A barking dog that says, "Good night,
Good night, good night to all."

Oh, these are the games that Baby plays
With those who love his baby ways.

SO BIG

By Esther Wilkin

How big is Baby?

Is Baby as big
As a ladybug
    Walking on a marigold leaf?

My Baby's bigger
Than a ladybug
    Walking on a marigold leaf.

Is Baby as big
As a caterpillar
Crawling along
        in a brown, woolly coat?

My Baby's bigger
Than a caterpillar
Crawling along
in a brown, woolly coat.

Is Baby as big
As a butterfly
  Flying in the pansy bed?

My Baby's bigger
Than a butterfly
  Flying in the pansy bed.

Is Baby as big
As a green grasshopper
Hopping about in the grass?

My Baby's bigger
Than a green grasshopper
   Hopping about in the grass.

Is Baby as big
As a pigeon
      Peck, peck, pecking in the park?

My Baby's bigger
Than a pigeon
Peck, peck, pecking in the park.

Is Baby as big
As a squirrel
  Sitting in the crab apple tree?

My Baby's bigger
Than a squirrel
   Sitting in the crab apple tree.

Is Baby as big
As a duck
    Swimming in the pond?

My Baby's bigger
Than a duck
    Swimming in the pond.

Is Baby as big
As a kitten
 Playing with a paper
  on a string?

My Baby's bigger
Than a kitten
 Playing with a paper
  on a string.

Is Baby as big
As a puppy
    Barking at a toad
      in the grass?

My Baby's bigger
Than a puppy
    Barking at a toad
        in the grass.

If my Baby's bigger
Than a ladybug,

Bigger than a caterpillar

or a butterfly,

Bigger than a
green grasshopper,

Bigger than a pigeon

or a squirrel,

Bigger than a duck

or a kitten

or a puppy—

Then how big IS Baby?

Baby is SOoooooooo Big!

THE BOY
WITH A DRUM

By David L. Harrison

There once was boy
With a little toy drum—
Rat-a-tat-tat-a-tat
Rum-a-tum-tum.

One day he went marching
And played on his drum—
Rat-a-tat-tat-a-tat
Rum-a-tum-tum.

Soon he was joined
By a friendly old cat—
Rum-a-tum-tum-a-tum
Rat-a-tat-tat.

Next they were joined
By a green spotted frog
Who sat by the road
On an old brown log.

And then they were joined
By a big yellow dog
Who marched down the road
With the green spotted frog.

They marched by a field,
They marched by a house—
And were joined by a cow
And a furry brown mouse.

They marched by a horse
Who was pulling a plow,
And he trotted behind them
And followed the cow.

Next they were joined
By a big white duck
And an old mother chicken
With a cluck-cluck-cluck.

And a pig and a goose
And a billy goat, too,
And a big red rooster
With a cock-a-doodle-doo.

And they all went marching
With a rat-a-tat-tat,
The boy with his drum
And the big friendly cat.

The horse and the cow
And the mouse and the dog,
The duck and the chicken
And the pig and the frog.

The goose and the rooster
And the billy goat, too,
With a baaa, honk, quack,
And a cock-a-doodle-doo,

The horse and the cow
And the mouse and the dog,
The duck and the chicken
And the pig and the frog.

The goose and the rooster
And the billy goat, too,
With a baaa, honk, quack,
And a cock-a-doodle-doo,

Oink, bow-wow, and a
Moo-moo-moo,
Neigh, cluck, squeak,
And a mew-mew-mew.

They all marched away
To the top of a hill—
If they haven't stopped marching,
They'll be marching still.

About
Eloise Wilkin

In a career that spanned sixty years, award-winning artist Eloise Wilkin illustrated close to one hundred children's books—well over half of them for Golden Books. She is known for her delicate watercolors, cherubic babies and children, and an unfailing sense of the innocence of childhood.

Born in Rochester, New York, in 1904, Eloise Wilkin studied art at the Rochester Institute of Technology, then moved to New York City. In 1944, after illustrating children's books for a number of different publishers, she signed an exclusive contract with Golden Books, for whom she proceeded to illustrate an average of one book every three months.

Earlier the artist had taken a ten-year break from her frantic pace as an illustrator to marry and to raise four children in a big, bustling house in Rochester, overlooking Canandaigua Lake. She and her sister Esther, with whom she was very close, married men who were, in fact, brothers. Eloise resumed work when Esther Wilkin wrote a children's story and presented it to Eloise to illustrate. The two Wilkins followed that book up with a number of successful collaborations.

The beloved house in Rochester, the family dog, Eloise's children (and later her grandchildren), all served as models for her books. In later years she used an instant camera to capture the youngsters' images. As she put it, "The children wouldn't sit still long enough to be sketched."

A few years before her death in 1987, Eloise Wilkin was asked if she enjoyed her work. "I don't like the deadlines," she answered, "but I love my work. When I'm doing a picture, I enter into it myself and stay till I'm done."